PLANETOID AMBER
—AND THE—
SPACE VILLAGE

RONALD DEAN DURBIN

ISBN: 978-1-63950-311-7 (sc)
ISBN: 978-1-63950-312-4 (e)

Writers Apex

Gateway Towards Success

8063 MADISON AVE #1252
Indianapolis, IN 46227
+13176596889
www.writersapex.com

FOREWORD

Travis Sky worked for the government (NaSA) listening center. His job was to listen and report anything unusual. One of NASA's satellites had malfunctioned and shot out into deep space. On occasion, it would send back data about items it passed. Today, it showed a picture of a large body moving in the direction of earth. Then, it crashed into the planetoid. The object was nearly as large as earth and was on a collision course for earth in 90 days more or less.

Travis quickly shot the information to his boss who sent it on up to the D.C. office. Miguel Sanchez couldn't believe his eyes. A big rock was heading towards earth. He had 90 days before it would arrive. He called Hector Lopez, of the President's staff, to tell them. Soon, he was on his way to meet with Ron Jared, Secretary of State and the President, Lindsey Graham.

Before crashing into the planetoid, Travis had taken a bunch of photos of the planetoid. Hector Lopez had already received twenty-five photos of the yet unnamed planetoid.

H ello. My name is Megan Boone. I'm a thirty-year-old Master Sergeant in the Air Force. Today is March 17, 2042. It's been eight years since Planetoid Amber passed by earth. The last eight years have been really hard on us, but we are all moving forward. After a ninety-day notice, the planetoid named Amber started its entry into the earth's atmosphere. For twenty minutes, it slowly passed by earth, sucking out the atmosphere into a cone like shape. Like poles caused it to bounce off earth. For a little while, we had too little air for humans and many animals to survive. Everything stopped unless it was using electricity to run on. Electromagnetic pulses, EMP, stopped all motors. The earth kept spinning, but the globe rotated just a little.

Amber kept on going. The Sun couldn't stop its projectory. In twenty minutes, Amber had changed our lives on earth forever. We are still adjusting. The science people are estimating that Amber kept twenty percent of our atmosphere. The rest came back to circle us once again.

Let me tell you about our globe. Now, all of Texas and the gulf coast have become tropical. Montana and the Dakotas have moved south and much of frozen Canada has started thawing. On the other side of the globe, Asia has gotten very cold. Much of Argentina has begun freezing.

Those few needing O_2 to survive would not pass out. Everyone else would. The older population did not wake up. That would include most of the American politicians. Only those around fifty or less would recover. Too many babies did not wake up.

After a lot of tears, recovery began. Back then, the military ordered Martial Law. Almost all of the higher-ranking generals had perished. I'm told, those generals left, met at the pentagon to work out a plan. First on the agenda had to be selecting the officer in charge or the Chief of the Joint Chiefs. Major General Richard Asherton was selected to be the new leader. Next, Vice Admiral Joshua Saladin was chosen to be in charge of the Navy and at that time the Marines and the Coast Guard. Brigadier General Manuel Breuer was selected to be the Chief of the Army with Brigadier General Susan Bolden becoming the Chief of the Air Force. Ronald Anders was selected to become the commander of Space Command. All of these were then promoted to full general (O-10, 4 stars).

Next, all of the services broke into groups. For example, the Air Force selected who would lead the different commands. Each command required a four-star general to lead it. The Air Force generals started with the Air Education and Training command, selecting Brigadier General Braxton Smith to be its new chief. Each command slot required a four-star general and they were all promoted.

After those decisions, the military left to run their commands. For example, AETC stopped all training. Flight training was stopped and the international pilots were allowed to fly their new aircraft to their home nations. Most training switched to "On the job training, OJT." All Security Force personnel were sent to their duty stations to continue their training. Even language training was discontinued. Some training would happen later, while other training would only happen at the individual bases. That then freed up all aircraft to be used to transport VIPs.

All of our reserve military units were activated. I lived in Wright City, Missouri right next to St. Louis. So for me, I reported to Scott AFB just east of St. Louis. My twin brothers Wes and Matt had just finished a four-year enlistment with the Navy. They were recalled to Virginia Beach and active duty. They had been aircraft mechanics, but the Navy would use them in a verity of jobs for now.

The military worked with local police officials, but the military was running the country. Each state has two sets of reserves. One is federal. The other, the National Guard, belongs to the state first and then the nation. So, the National Guard stayed at home to help out locally.

The first task at hand was to record the dead and cremate their remains. There were too many dead in America to have funerals. Bodies were brought to the center of each city and cremated there. Officials recorded their names and then burned the bodies.

Life in America froze for the next several weeks. Properties needed to be passed on. Businesses needed to figure out who the boss was. The science people tell us that in America alone, more than 60,000,000 did not wake up.

Tidal water surged as high as one hundred feet and stayed there for some time. Most of Florida went under water. Slowly, what had been Florida drained, but it was not the same. Most all of Miami was gone. Many coastal cities had washed away. The Keys were gone. Parks like Walt Disney World were only skeletons of what had been. Virtually all of the beach homes were gone. Beach hotels were gone along with most businesses located on the shoreline.

The rest of the Gulf coast changed as well. Several coastal cities were gone. New Orleans was closer to the gulf now and Galveston was gone. Houston had been covered with fifty feet of water and now had a bay. Corpus Christi and Padre Island were gone. Up north, Manhattan had been covered with a hundred feet of water, but it stayed. The East River would stay in its same place. Inland, the Mississippi rose and went back to its banks, as did the Missouri.

Prices dropped on everything. It would take months before houses could be legally freed up. Nothing was sold. My twin brothers and I moved into our parent's home. They didn't wake up. People were just told to wait. After getting our families settled in, we left to our different locations of active duty.

The military helped get food moving again. As highways were cleared of vehicles, sergeants drove the eighteen-wheelers to get food to the stores. In Texas, the bigger stores like Walmart and HEB had enough drivers. But, smaller stores also needed supplies.

On the roadway, those found dead inside their vehicles were identified and removed by the military. Families were notified when possible. Next, the bodies were taken to the closest city and cremated. Their autos were taken to large fields for storage, until they could be claimed. Because of the high tides, many individuals were just never found.

In the United States, there was calm. In many other countries, there was a great deal of chaos. All around the world leadership was changing. Bad people saw this as a great opportunity to set themselves up as their country's leaders. Riots occurred as did revolutions. For now, the United States could not help out. We were busy just trying to survive.

For right now, the United States did not have borders. In the south, anyone wanting to go north could. In the north, anyone wanting to go south could. Mexico was one of those countries where bad people saw a chance to cease power. These people killed anyone disagreeing with their leadership. So, we were not stopping people from going north.

With all of the flooding, what once was, was no more. Farms had to wait for their property to drain and then see what still worked. A lot of equipment had been covered with water for weeks. Hay had gone bad. Livestock were missing or dead. Life would recover. It would just take time to sort things out.

When all of this happened, my reserve unit was activated and I put on the uniform of a Security Policeman. We are called Security Forces. So, I know that in the US military, an officer would normally make 0-6, colonel, around his fortieth birthday. Four or five years later, he would become a new general, 0-7 or brigadier. Then in a couple of years, he might pin on another star. A and 0-10 or four star general would pin on in his early fifties. We lost almost all of our three-star generals, except for Vice Admiral Joshua Saladin. A few of our two-star generals didn't wake up as well.

My brothers Wes and Matt had served together in the Navy for four years and were now recalled to active duty. They didn't mind. It gave them a solid income and kept them busy. They were both told to report to Virginia Beach. They stayed at the base there and not on a ship. For right now, their jobs were to keep aircraft flying. At that time the Federal Aviation Administration, the FAA, had shut down all of our airports.

Personally, I had been an E-4 and was promoted to E-5 and today to E-7, or Master Sergeant. My new job was to help keep congress safe. Congress pretty much died. No senators woke up. Only five congressmen would survive. William George had just been re-elected to the house. The other four were first-termers. They were Alice Morales of New Mexico; Angelina Vasquez of California; Mike Shertz of Missouri; and Anthony Hopkins of New York.

General Richard Asherton had been selected to be the Chief of the Joint Chiefs. He declared Martial Law. He then asked Congressman Bill George to become the President of the United States. General Asherton hoped new elections could be held within a few years. But for now, Bill George was the President.

Reservists had been activated, including me. We were given one week to take care of family issues and then report in at our nearest base. Once again, rank had to be bumped up. Most reservists were older than those on active duty. No generals survived, so colonels were all given one star for now. Lieutenant colonels were all promoted to full colonel and so on. The enlisted ranks lost all of our E-8s and E-9s.

Next, states, counties, and cities needed to set up local governments. Each state did things their own way. In New Mexico and New York, their congressmen came home to become their governors. In California and Missouri, those congressmen came home to help with the transition but did not accept their states' leadership.

Hundreds of thousands of autos needed to get moved to temporary locations until owners could be matched up. Forklifts were brought in just to move the autos off the roadways. All towing companies were asked to help out. They would get a credit for each vehicle they brought in.

Police would also promote up those waiting in line. General Asherton gave the police permission to fill all vacancies.

Next, hospitals seemed to have about half of the personnel they needed to function. They just simply had to make do with what they had for the time being. Many doctors were older and did not wake up. The staff was permitted to make adjustments. Younger doctors were put in charge over all, but nurses would be running the floors. Medical technicians were suddenly in charge of floors as well.

Once again, Congressman Bill George from Colorado was sworn in as the President. Congresswoman Alice Morales was sworn in as the Governor of New Mexico. Congressman Anthony Hopkins was sworn in as the Governor of New York. Congressmen Mike Shertz and Angelina Vasquez were flown home on Air Force aircraft and helped their states set up new leadership, but would then return to DC to take care of government business. We didn't have any others. No Supreme Court justices survived. There were many things like that that needed to be taken care of.

In combat situations, choppers are used to go even a few miles. General Asherton executed this plan for now. He used one to get over to the Pentagon in Arlington, Virginia. Once there, he set up a chain of command. For the military, this was a normal procedure in difficult times. General Asherton had been selected to the position as the Chief.

Air Force One flew President George to Washington. There, he had a shell of positions to fill. All he had to do was to place people into positions that already existed. Each support position already had a staff in place; President George needed to officially stamp what those offices were already doing. His own chief of staff was his campaign manager, Mary Bradley. She became Secretary of State. His Secretary of Defense, Ronald Jefferies, had been an Under-Secretary for budgets.

Next, President George needed a Vice-President. He was turned down by both Schertz and Vasquez. They chose to stay on the outside and help form the Cabinet. In the meantime, Jere Bell from Illinois accepted the position of Vice-President. Jere had been an undersecretary in Homeland Security.

Now, Bill George, Mike Schertz, Angelina Vasquez, and Jere Bell sat down to discuss what Americans needed the most:

1. Water,

2. Food,

3. Housing,

4. Money,

5. Gas,

6. Legal help (Property, cars, homes, jobs, ownership),

7. Law and order (functioning govt)

Next, Bill George called his Cabinet into a one-week workshop. They would stay four weeks. Well sort of. He didn't have a Cabinet, so he called for the three senior people from each section and a secretary from each section. Also, he had decided to record the meeting so there would be no doubting what had been decided. Offices of:

1. Vice-President: Jere Bell, plus 3

2. Chief of Staff:

3. Sec of State:

4. Sec of Defense:

5. Attorney General:

6. Treasury:

7. Office of Management & Budget:

8. Council of Economic Advisers:

9. Office of Sci & Tech:

10. EPA:

11. Transportation:

12. Labor:

13. Interior:

14. Commerce:

15. Agriculture:

16. Education:

17. Homeland Security:

18. Veterans Affairs:

19. United Nations rep:

20. US trade rep:

21. Small Business Administration:

22. Sec of Energy:

23. Mike Schertz of Missouri

24. Angelina Vasquez of California

General Ronald Anders took over Space Command. His biggest problem was his Space Station. It was gone. The Moon Village Space Station was gone. It was traveling with Amber. Eight of the twelve support rockets were ready to launch with four more being prepared. General Anders decided that it was now the Amber Village. It took five days to prepare, but he began launching his Village support rockets. He could launch one every twenty-four hours. By then, numbers nine and ten were ready to go and were launched. They would all follow Amber.

On the Space station, twelve astronauts had to figure out what was next for them. Six ladies and six men sat down to talk about Next. Nine would stay with the station and three would return to earth. The space station had three escape pods that could re-enter earth's atmosphere.

Amy Peterson, Brian Zule, and David Cook entered the pod and shot back towards earth. It was like a mini-RV. They had no idea how long it would take to reach earth, but they started. They had enough food and water for one year. (The water would include recycled urine.)

Those staying on the space station included Aina Turnbek and her sister, Mica Turnbek, both of whom were medical doctors. Verna Smart was the pilot with Chip Aldrin working as her Co. Judy Long and Anara Flowers were botanists. The other three were engineers, Allen Olde, Scott Pike, and Jason Pierce. Rank and country no longer mattered.

When the time was right, they would land on Amber. They were now not part of any country. Today was March 20, 0001. For now, they would still have seven days in a week. There was no hurry to do anything more. Time didn't matter. The day would still be 24 hours. The team was just along for the ride to wherever Amber took them. For now, they would still call their planet Amber.

The best way to think about or picture the space station would be to think about a clock. The space station was a large flat disc. It had been built over several years. At the top would be a twelve. Moving to the right you would have a one, then two, then three on around to twelve again at the top. Along the outside edge, were 60 rooms or cells.

The first nine rooms were already taken by the current crew. Each room was furnished with: hot and cold running water; a sofa bed; sheets and pillows; a clock; two lounge chairs; intercom; large TV; attached was a bathroom with a small shower; mirror; sink; chair; a drawer with shaving stuff; a manicure kit; hair brush and hair dryer; and of course towels and wash clothes. Each room was set up like an efficiency apartment. You would find a tall fridge for fresh and frozen foods; a sink; a dishrack; cabinets; pots and pans; a skillet; hot pads with dishes for six. Each room was sealed and waiting for occupants. Each could be expanded if needed for children that would come in the future.

In the center of our clock, was a lobby. From the center lobby to the 12, was a hallway. From the center lobby to the 3 was a hallway. Yes, from the center lobby to the 6 was a hallway. Same for the 9. Down each hallway were stores, like at a mini-mall. In the center lobby area, you have a Bar/ Club. A Café was next to it. Also in the center, you have a Gym and a grocery store. All of the units were closed and ready to open as soon as the Village landed. On top of the space station were 12 connections or docking platforms for the rockets that would come.

For now, on the village space station, the nine were alone and didn't know if that would ever change. For now, everything was free and no money was exchanged.

The Village had sixty rooms for living quarters. There were large walkways going north, south, east and west. In the center of the mall area were the most important stores. You would find the club and café, a spa, a grocery store, a chapel, the clinic, and moving out down the pathways, were other stores for when there would have been people living and staying on the station. In the future, there would have been several stores along with three laundromats. Most of those stores were now closed and sealed. One laundromat was open for the nine. The clinic was open because of Aina and Mica. The bar was open for the nine and everything was free.

The nine would just wait for now. If Amber hooked up with a star, then they would open the village and go forward. Babies would be needed in order to continue their existence. That time hadn't come yet. The club was a good place to wait and talk. Within the club, Verna had an office. Chip also had one connected with Verna's. Across the hall was the clinic with Aina and Mica. Down the hall, Judy and Anara had plants. One day they would have hundreds of plants. Next to them Allen, Scott, and Jason ran the hardware store. The other shops would have to wait for other people to open them.

Amy, Brian, and David were heading in the direction of earth. Their pod could survive for a year. Today, April 1, 2034, they were just worrying about today.

Back on earth, people were dealing with what is. America was a capitalist country. Today, money would not be changing hands. All credit cards were cancelled. The auto industry shut down. Dealerships would need to stay open to service their brands. The housing industry shut down. People were trying to figure out what was Next.

The government was supporting all banks and credit unions with cash. All credit card debt had to be forgiven. For now, everything had to be handled with cash. The military had a credit card system that was still functioning. The military left their weapons in the armory. Every soldier was out trying to get life back to normal. Groceries were being shipped. Bodies and autos were being taken care of. Identifications were being made. It would take weeks for all of this to happen.

I mentioned that my parents didn't wake up. They were cremated, but my family gathered together for a memorial dinner at their home. Officials saw that nobody was homeless. If there was not an empty home, then they were taken to a shelter.

For now, no house payments were due. The government told everyone that they had six months to figure out what they were going to do. For many, it was a time to return home. My brothers and I returned to our parent's home. Our families brought what they could carry. Then we left our families there and reported for our military duty.

Those in the auto industry lost their jobs, so they returned home.

The housing industry shut down, so those folks returned home.

People needed time to grieve. Working and making more money would just have to wait.

On the twelfth day after leaving the village, Amy picked up an image of a rocket heading in their direction.

On earth, that would have been April 1, 2034. She was able to communicate with it. "Hello."

"Yes. Is this the village?"

"No. You have Amy. Who am I speaking with?"

"Ok. The Amy I know was supposed to be living on the Village. Amy, this is Kory Hutter."

"I'm in a pod heading back to earth with Brian and David. The rest of our team is on the space station. Amber hijacked us. The other nine are going along for the ride. What are you doing out here?"

"We are trying to catch up to the space station. I'm commander of the Alpha rocket with your supplies."

"Amazing. We don't need anything, just keep on trucking. Who's with you?"

"Barb Walsh is my Co. Jen Still and Charlie Cash are along for the ride. We are called Alpha. Bravo was to launch the next day and so on. We have been allocated twelve rockets, but only eight were ready."

"We left the Village twelve days ago. Keep on going. Bye for now."

"Roger that. Out here."

Kory was not happy with still being so far away from the Village. He fired his rockets and gave his ship another blast. He hoped he could speed up some and reach the Village. Kory was not in touch with the other ships. He knew he was on his own.

Back on earth, in several countries, bad people had ceased power for now and were having a good time. The United States was at peace. We were just slowly moving forward. Again, our borders were open. People were just trying to eat. Families came together to see who was still among the living.

The President's cabinet was busy working on what was next. For now:

1. Water would be free.

2. Food chains had to stay open. Debit cards could be used for now.

3. Housing: People needed places to sleep. Families could keep their parents homes with no taxes.

4. Banks: Everyone would be issued a debit card to use until things could get figured out. People were still responsible for what they spent.

5. Gas: Debit cards were accepted at all gas stations.

6. Legal help: Services were rendered at no cost for now. Those charges would come as credits from the government.

7. Law officers were working twelve hours a day to keep everything calm.

Back on the pod, another rocket came into radar. Amy asked for their ID. "Hello."

"Yes. Hello. Is this the Village?"

"No, we were on the station, but now we're heading back to earth. I have David and Brian with me. The other nine are on the Village, going wherever it's going. Alpha rocket passed here twelve hours ago. He fired his booster rockets to get more speed."

Ten rockets in all were launched. They all carried supplies that would be needed in the future. They were:

1. Pilot and Co; solar stuff; worker clothes; space suits; and AI stuff.

2. Pilot and Co; two electric Humvees for ground travel; mechanics to work on them; supplies for the autos

3. Pilot and Co; two botanists; AI stuff; food; live and frozen plants; more solar stuff.

4. Pilot and Co; general supplies; botanists; water; soil; gardening tools.

5. Pilot and Co; two more workers; more water and mulch.

6. Pilot and Co; two more workers; fuel.

7. Pilot and Co; two more workers; frozen foods.

8. Pilot and Co; two more workers; baby animals; feed.

9. Pilot and Co; animal and human embryos (frozen).

10. Pilot and Co; baby supplies, baby clothes, formula, bottles, kids clothes, some toys, school materials.

Five months down the road, rockets started arriving at the village. Docking was done on autopilot. Once in the socket, they could be locked down. The Village residents were happy to see the newcomers. Life was no longer simple. The bank would need to open for a few hours each day. Cash was not used. Debit cards were. Nothing was free any longer. Prices were set and charged on their debit cards.

The bar was still the busiest place. But, other stores opened now. The chapel remained open and unlocked. Charlie Cash was a deacon in his church back on earth and kept watch over the chapel. The other stores had hours of operation. The village went from nine people to forty-nine.

At Space command, Gen. Anders was working out compensation for those families separated from their astronauts. Each family would receive $200,000 annually for five years. All of the astronauts were considered gone for good. Each would be considered dead. After five years, the payments would stop. Any spouse was now considered single. If any should return, the money would be kept by their families.

After six months, in September of 2034, the pod entered earth's atmosphere. "Hello Houston. This is David Cook. I'm in a pod from the Village. I have Amy Peterson and Brian Zule with me. Requesting permission to land at Kennedy."

"That's a go. Welcome back. How are you doing? What about the other nine?"

"They were good. We left six months ago. We are fine, also. Tired of this pod. I don't know how much help we'll need after being in space for so long. Just have a medical team standing by."

"Roger. Will do."

With that, the pod entered earth's atmosphere and began its plan for landing at the Kennedy Space Center.

With that short conversation, all of Space command was excited about their return. The President was notified that they were returning from the Village.

The cabinet met for those seven days and found it needed many more. Seven turned into forty. That was just the beginning. Then each agency set off on their own to deal with their specialty. Flying was impossible and driving was difficult to say the least. America was moving, but crawling. Food was getting to stores, but slowly. Quantities were very limited with frozen foods winning out.

Farmers and ranchers gathered those animals they could find. They drove tractors that they could get running and planted what they could. After a few months, fresh produce began arriving at stores. Eggs and milk took a little longer but they too began showing up. Meatpackers began shipping fresh goods as well.

The military began turning over driving supplies around to those civilians needing work. The work of the military could bring their people back into the bases. All of the coastal areas needed extra help getting back to normal. Actually, they would never get back to normal. They would just move forward.

Construction workers started rebuilding those places destroyed by the tides. Cash was tight, but the banks could loan money on debit cards. America began rebuilding.

In space, the Village started receiving ships. The station was a large flat disc. If you think of a clock, twelve would be at the top followed by one, two, three, etc. On the perimeter of the clock were twelve docking locks. As ships approached, they would jettison their engines. A large arm would hook onto them and bring them into their dock.

Verna was the overall commander of the village and would oversee each ship's docking. Her Co-Pilots would handle the actual docking. Each ship took a while to dock, so the time lapse was good. After one week, the village had ten rockets docked.

Next, each ship needed to go horizontal. Each ship was shaped like a cone. The pointed end was then laid down towards the center. Nothing was on the twelve with Alpha having been placed on the one. Bravo was placed on the two and then laid down. In the end, all ten ships were laid down and opened for operation.

On the station had been nine people, now there were forty-nine. Each person had their own room or cell. Life changed. Shops that had been prepared were now open. The bank had two tellers and it was only opened mornings. Crew members didn't have actual cash. They used debit cards.

Now it was time to land the Village onto Amber. Verna launched one of the two remaining pods to go and search for a flat place for the Village to anchor down.

Jason Pierce stayed at the hardware store while Allen Olde and Scott Pike entered the pod. Kory Hutter launched the pod and headed towards the surface of Amber. The only light came from the pod.

Amber appeared to be a big black rock. There were hills and valleys. The team found a flat field for the village to land on and notified Verna. It was not too high or down at the bottom of a mountain.

The village now became a flying saucer, space ship. The forty-six passengers took their seats and prepared to land on Amber. All ten ships were docked and locked down.

With that, the center rockets fired. The village came to the field and began landing vertically. As it set down, four pillars from the center mall came out like table legs. As the pillars touched down, twelve steel rods, spines, came out from the circumference. Chip Aldrin was operating the controls and could level out the ship. After a couple of adjustments, the all clear was sounded. The village was now anchored on Amber.

Verna thought to herself, now we just need to find a star.

Starlight,

Star bright.

First star I see tonight.

I wish I may.

I wish I might.

Have the wish I wish tonight.

The name of the star will be BRIGHT.

Back on earth, the United States was getting settled. A lot of people had gone home. Whatever their dreams had been, now home seemed more important. Family seemed more important than money or power.

Mexico was in revolution. The bad people had seized power, but now the common person was rejecting their power. The military chose to go with the civilians. Bullets were flying. More people moved north into the U.S.

The United States of America was reforming. Earth had rotated a little, so what had been colder was now warming. All of the southern states had become tropical. Montana and the Dakotas were warmer.

Chip gave Jason Pierce the okay to start closing the Village ground level. Jason lowered two garage doors. One was at the three and the other was at the nine location. Next, the wench brought rolls of vinyl siding and began circling the village spines. The rolls were four feet in height, so it would take three trips around to cover the twelve-foot spines. It looked like a huge umbrella.

The vinyl siding was permanent. The village started with one floor. Then the ships were added to the top. Now, the ground floor gave the village three stories.

The ground floor would still need people to wear spacesuits. Still, there was no heat on the ground floor. The Humvees could be kept there as well as the pods. The garage doors were eight feet tall and could open and close. Special tape was used with the vinyl connecting to the garage doorframes.

Aina and Mica had opened the clinic by themselves. Now, they had two medical technicians helping them. The clinic had a reception room and five examination rooms. Beyond those were a surgical room and a recovery room.

Today, they would begin In vitro fertilization on themselves. Babies would be needed if the village was to be successful. Baby embryos were in storage, but would need to be placed into a womb. That started today with both doctors.

You don't just put the embryos into the womb. Medicine can make the body think it is pregnant. Then on day six, the embryos can be inserted into the womb. Once in the womb, the embryos would need to connect with the wall and continue developing. Then in nine months, a baby would be ready.

Both doctors chose baby girls. Now the process started. Two baby girls would grow. Now, April of year 02. Baby girls would begin the new third year.

Back on earth, after twelve months of Marshall Law, General Asherton was ready to begin switching to Civilian controls. He met with President Bill George and so the process began.

States would replace their senators and representatives. It was suggested that a Democrat refill a former Democrat's slot. For example, in Texas they sent thirty-eight delegates to the House. Thirteen were Democrats with twenty-five Republicans. Six states would only be sending one person to the House of Representatives. Each state needed to send two senators. For now, all would serve until 2040. In 2040, the slots or positions would revert to the original model. Senators serve six years and face re-election. Representatives serve two years and face re-election.

In Washington DC, offices already had staffs in place. The states just needed to choose those people to fill the leadership positions. Elections could be held in 2039 to refill those positions. A presidential election would go along with these.

Fighting was still going on in several countries. Mexico was still not a safe place to be. People were still moving north.

In Europe, the royal families helped settle things down. Advice was given and taken. Parliaments continued to function. In Asia, things looked pretty much the same. China had a structure set up that backfilled positions. In Russia, people were in place to replace those lost. Africa was in revolution. South of Mexico, fighting was going on for political control of the different nations.

On Amber Village, life was settling in. Shops were opening and people were carrying on as if they had been there forever. Verna had been the commander with Chip being her second. They both kept offices connected to the club. For now, they would continue their leadership positions.

When a person goes into the military, someone decides what jobs are given out. Yes, qualifications are required, but so is a vacancy. Judy, Chip, Kory, and Anara met to fill all of the slots. A person just needed to get close to being qualified.

Store clerks required an interest in the store. There wasn't a Walmart, but there was a Homemart. Five clerks were sent to it. It had several different departments. Most people had to work at more than one store. The workday was two five-hour shifts.

On earth in January of 2037, Congress was back in session. Budgets needed to be worked on. The money issue was a problem and needed to be worked on. The President named nine new judges for the Supreme Court. These individuals would need to be approved.

In September of 02, on the Village, life was moving forward. The two doctors were pregnant. Some farm animals were now large enough to butcher. Others were impregnated to begin life again. Judy and Anara had plants growing in the mall fields.

Everyone was still waiting on a star. That changed. After two and a half years, a star was seen. Still far off, but seen.

Then on January thirteenth of year three, Mica gave birth to her baby girl weighing seven pounds and eight ounces. She was twenty inches in length. Her name was Hope. The ladies had been lucky. They were the only doctors on the Village. If there had been any complications with the births then who would deal with the situation? So, there were no complications and the births came through the birth canals.

Hope changed the emotions of everyone. It's like going from black and white to color. The response to her birth was amazing.

Then on the twenty-sixth, Aina delivered her little girl, Adelina. She was eight pounds and one ounce, also twenty inches in length. The baby girls came to work with their moms at the clinic. The doctors always had someone stopping by to see these miracles.

On the Village, the babies changed the atmosphere. Life was now very positive. Now, others wanted babies in their lives. Some matched up with a partner while others did In vitro. On earth, it would have cost one hundred thousand dollars. On the Village, there was no charge. It was important to continue growing the population. Between now and year five, the Village would see fifteen more births.

Individual rooms were now expanded to house the seventeen new babies. Hope and Adelina changed the Village in a positive way.

Star Bright was getting closer and hopes were getting higher.

On earth, by 2038 life had settled down. You can't go back, so you go forward as best as you can. Coastal areas had started rebuilding. The auto industry was still shut down. Stores had the food that they needed.

People were still moving north to get away from the destruction that had been caused by the revolution. Mexico was now at peace, but the damage had been done. In Central and South America, life was calmer. Europe was churning and happy. Asia was working pretty well. Africa was still smoking. Fighting was on going.

Megan Boone here. We've had no contact with the Village. We hope the best for them. Here on earth, things have changed a lot. The gulf coast is now tropical. Canada is having a great time with the weather change in temperatures. Mexico has settled down. The US is helping with rebuilding. Actually, it's cheaper than having thousands of new immigrants. Africa is pretty settled down now. Asia is doing okay.

Elections were held in 2039 and anyone wanting to stay in congress was re-elected. The President was given one more term. Cities were figuring out what they needed to do to continue.

In year six, Star Bright was now about a year away! Now with seventeen new babies, the Village was alive with hope for the future. Animals were grazing in the mall fields. Milk was being given by our cows. Lamb and goat meat was available. Cheese was also being made fresh. Frozen commodities were in plenty, but one day they would be gone. Fresh products were always better and prolonged or extended our supplies.

By the year 04, the Village had welcomed seventeen new humans. Of those, seven came by natural sex. The seven couples decided that they wanted to legally marry. The Village didn't have a licensed minister, but Charlie Cash was a deacon in his church back in Texas. He agreed to become a licensed minister for the Village. Verna gave her new minister his legal license to perform ministerial necessities.

In 04, the seven couples agreed to marry at the chapel. Now, Pastor Cash would join all seven at the same ceremony. Also beginning now, Pastor Cash would begin holding traditional Sunday worship services.

The Village had sixty rooms. For now, forty-nine were individual rooms. They could be joined. For those seven, they moved to rooms that had a connecting door. Now their apartment doubled in size. Verna decided that any couple wanting to live together could, but they would need to become legal couples to get the connecting rooms.

To begin with, the seven couples started with rooms sixty and fifty-nine. Then came fifty-eight and fifty-seven. The double rooms didn't change the overall count. They just opened the door between them.

NEW COUPLES AND ROOMS

60, 59 – Quin, Shelly, Eva

58, 57 – Terry, Nancy, Gail

56, 55 – Abe, Pam, Hank

54, 53 – Rodger, Ayana, Wendy

52, 51 – Bob, Alicia, Victor

50, 49 – Mike, Albina, Tommy

48, 47 – Adam, Zena, David

The Space Station had been in the works for twenty years. We were only two years away from having it completed. The plan was to then land it on the moon for a permanent community to live and work there. Pieces of the space station had been sent into orbit over the last seven years. Twelve rockets were planned to resupply the station.

Then Amber changed all of that. Amber took the Space Village and twelve astronauts with her as she passed earth. Now it has become the Amber Village. Ten of the original dozen ships were sent chasing Amber. Now the Village is anchored on Amber.

Years before, several ladies had agreed to save their eggs and mate them with sperm to create baby humans. Most of the embryos would not mature to the right developmental stage. Those that did were then saved, cryogenics. Mica and Aina had three good embryos each. They each used one. After six years in space, Amber now had seventeen new babies. Ten of the babies came from In Vitro. Seven happened the old-fashioned way.

For each of the new parents, life as they had known it, changed. Most parents used a combination of breast feeding and formula. As was the case with Mica and Aina. Their baby girls changed their work schedule. I should say their whole life's schedule (laugh out loud). Hope and Adelina slept most of the night but, they would wake up and require attention several times each night. This extended their sleep time. By 0900, they were ready to get up and get changed. Moms' private time went away. Poopy diapers needed to be changed each day, feeding happened every two hours, etc.

The baby girls slept in pajamas and had blankets, but the blankets would soon get kicked off. Sometimes the girls required space and at other times they needed to touch mom, snuggle.

Breakfast was cereal and later whatever mom ate. Rocket number ten carried baby and kid stuff, to include Gerber's baby food and Huggies diapers, enough for the next ten years. After that, the Village would need to revert to the way it used to be. Mom would use cloth diapers and blend her own food.

Now with kids, a schoolroom with a teacher was needed. Anara became the school director and teacher. She was also given the responsibility for the Daycare Center. Hope and Adelina would be the first to start school at four. They would be followed by the other fifteen.

So, the clinic opened up at 1100 each day for five hours. Hope and Adelina came to work with their moms. Now, one of the rooms became a nursery. Aina and Mica were always on call. Each took a week at a time. In all of the years of living on the Village, they had never been called.

Seventeen new humans were on Amber Village. Life was simple. The new babies required a great deal of attention.

When all of their biological needs had been met, you were just beginning. They needed a lot of attention.

Sixty-six humans now lived on Amber. Seventeen needed a lot of help. By two, Hope and Adelina were able to be alone together in their nursery there at the clinic. Cameras were always watching them to make sure they were safe. But that left fifteen little people needing a lot of attention and that was okay. There wasn't much else to do.

Now on Amber, male and female numbers were even, thirty-three. Of those thirty-three ladies, twenty-six were adults. Of those, six indicated they were no longer interested in getting pregnant. Mica and Aina would do it again in another year (07). Several others indicated they would be willing to get pregnant at least one more time.

In year seven, Hope and Adelina turned four. The other babies were in their twenties (months). Mica was pregnant again. She chose her other girl embryo. Aina was holding off a little.

Star Bright was now just weeks away. Life on Amber was brighter. Hope was building.

Amber Village had sixty rooms or cells for living. Of those, forty-nine were in use. Mica and Aina now had connecting rooms that had also been expanded for their two babies. The seven new couples had connecting rooms that had been expanded to make room for their new babies. There were eight additional ladies raising their babies in their single rooms, but those rooms had been expanded for the new children.

The normal workday on the Village was ten hours. Several positions were for five hours which meant they still owed five more hours somewhere else. For their first two years, raising a new baby counted as five hours.

So, Anara had left plants and farming to Judy. Judy had experts working with her so she wasn't required to know everything about her plants and animals. She just directed and monitored this portion of the village.

Anara became the new director of Education. She also set up the new Day Care where babies could be watched for no charge. This same area would be used for the new school classrooms. Now at four, Hope and Adelina were ready for school. Anara had agreed to become their teacher with four other workers joining her. In January of 07, classes would start with Hope and Adelina.

With two of her helpers, Anara entered ship number ten, Ship Juliet. Sets of twenty-five hardback books for all grades, including four-year-olds came with one hundred workbooks for each grade. At grade seven, books switched to a specific topic (i.e. biology, history, and math).

Ship Juliet would remain the warehouse for these until they would be needed. For now, Anara and her team would grab stuff for the first three years. The small electric truck was great help.

Anara had been selected as the Director for Teaching. She was to be the only full-time teacher with four part-time teachers. That soon changed with twenty-seven babies being born. Now she had four full-time teachers.

People were having a good time shopping at the baby store. Those without babies were shopping for those with babies. The rooms didn't come with kids' stuff. Parents did receive vouchers to pick up dishes, food products, and sleeping stuff (i.e. beds, PJs).

Finally, we entered Star Bright's orbit. For the first time, the Village had normal daylight. The Bar was a busy place with people celebrating. It was a good reason to celebrate.

I HAVE MY WISH TONIGHT.

Scott Pike was the engineer in charge of the power plant. He directed what happened there, but he didn't stay at the power plant. Scott had four full-time workers with at least one of them always being at the power plant. Scott chose to spend his time at the hardware store.

Back on earth, life was going forward. Car dealerships began merging and or closing. General Motors was in good shape and actually bought one of the Korean auto companies. Ford was able to hang on to what it had. Others merged with either European or Japanese companies in order to survive.

New homes were not being built yet, but the construction industry survived by rebuilding those businesses destroyed by the flooding. Congress was working hard to go forward with what we had. State, county, and city governments were working from within to get everything back online.

Businesses decided who would be the next boss. For wealthy family-owned businesses, the families decided who would be their next head or leader. Corporations reworked their leadership and director boards. Life was moving forward.

Farms were back in business. You can't worry about what had been lost. They just went forward with planting and with the animals that survived.

On January 12 of 07, Mica delivered her second daughter. Erin was twenty-one inches long and weighed eight pounds.

Aina knew it was now time for her to get pregnant again. Eight other ladies joined her in the process. Four were doing so for the first time with four more repeating the In Vitro process. So, at the end of 07 or the beginning of 08, Amber Village would have ten new babies. That would bring the total count to seventy-six people living in Amber Village.

Before, Kory and Jason had been out exploring and mapping with a Hummer, but the only light had come from them. Now with light from Bright, they could travel safely, anywhere. Exploring would become a daily task.

On their next trip out, Verna came along. She wanted to see what they were all living on.

Back on earth, life in the United States was getting back to normal. President George got his Supreme Court Justices approved, so the Supreme court was now back and working. He also signed for the nation's first budget in eight years. On Capitol Hill, the democrats and republicans were each blaming each other for Amber's damage.

Tens of thousands of autos remained unclaimed. The states made deals with the former auto dealerships to get rid of them. They could take them on consignment or just buy them outright. On consignment meant they would share the resell money with the state. Buying the autos outright meant that they were taking a chance on selling the autos, but all of the profit would be theirs.

Unclaimed homes went pretty much the same way. If they were located within the city limits, then the city council would handle the resell. If not, then the county government would handle the details of the resell.

The long war in Ukraine ended because the Old Guard that had wanted to see the old Soviet Union reborn died. Their younger replacements wanted to see a stronger Russia. Russian troops pulled out of Ukraine. Zelensky brokered a cease-fire. Both sides were happy.

The Crimea remained independent.

Africa had changed a little bit. South Africa broke up into ten little countries. Europe looked pretty much the same. Asia had settled down and was recovering.

On December 21 of 07, Diva was born to Aina. She weighed eight pounds and three ounces and was twenty-one inches long. Over the next five months, eight more babies added to Amber's population now totaling 76.

Humvees were not the only electric vehicles on Amber Village. There were four small electric trucks that stayed in the mall area. They carried things; cleaned walkways; and carried trash. Also, there were five electric golf carts. A few people had electric wheels. Others used skateboards to go from place to place.

In 07, Anara opened the Amber school. Hope and Adelina were her first two students. They got together for four hours daily. The school was located right next to the daycare. In 08, fifteen little people began school. Now seventeen little people were in school. Hope and Adelina were in kindergarten with the others in four-year-old classes.

Amber Village started with nine astronauts. Then ten ships brought supplies and forty new humans. Then Mica and Aina gave birth to Hope and Adelina. Next fifteen ladies decided to get pregnant. Then, you were up to sixty-six humans in the Village. Next, we had ten more babies, bringing the total up to seventy-six humans living in the Village. Seven couples married after their babies arrived. Still, just forty-nine of the sixty rooms are occupied.

Several stores have opened. The three laundromats are busy places. Anara has started two grades in her school. Next door to her school is the free day care center opened sixteen hours a day with four full-time workers.

Still, the busiest place is the Bar.

Albert Baker was running the power plant full-time. He came to the clinic for his annual physical. He was excited to be there to see Mica. He was shown to his examination room and checked out by the medical technician. Next, Mica came in to speak with him. "Albert, you are looking good. All of your tests came back positive. Do you have any questions for me?"

"Yes. Can I help you take care of Hope and Erin?"

Stunned, Mica replied, "I'm sorry, I don't understand."

"I'm saying that I want to be around you and your kids."

Mica thought for a moment. Then she grabbed Albert by his shirt and pulled him close. "You mean like this?" Then she kissed him.

Albert was surprised by her response and then held her. "Yes."

In June of 08, Albert and Mica joined two other couples in another wedding ceremony at the chapel.

Mica moved out of her cell, #3 and moved into a non-used cell, #46, with Albert moving in next to her in #45. Then they did the kid expansion with a door connecting both efficiency apartments. Now Aina was raising her two little ladies on her own.

The Bar and Café had started off as separate, but Ronnie Dean merged the two. Now he had five full-time workers to take care of the Village people. It was now time for his annual checkup. So, he saw Aina. He was shown into a prep room. They took his blood pressure and weight. Ronnie was the oldest Village member. The Village astronauts had been with Amber for eight years. Ronnie came to the station at thirty and was now forty.

Aina greeted the oldest member of the Village with good news. "Ok Doctor Dean. All of your tests have come back positive. You are looking good for another year. Do you have any questions for me?"

"Yes. I understand that you are now raising your two daughters alone?"

"Yes. Mica said good-bye. She's moved in with Albert. They were married by Pastor Cash last week."

"Can I say hello?"

"I'm sorry. I don't understand."

"I'm saying I want to help you raise your two daughters. Can I move into Mica's apartment?"

"That's being saved for their new father, when I find him."

"Duh."

Ronnie moved into #3. Pastor Cash had another wedding. The Village now had eleven couples. Twenty-two of the forty-nine were now couples. Twenty-five were still single. Twenty-seven babies have been born in the Village.

Jason began the final phase of construction on the Village when he guided the wench to unroll solar panels onto the top of the Village structure. A power line now ran to the power plant. The power plant then reduced its output to match what was needed on the Village.

Back on earth, life was moving forward. In the United States, life was almost normal again. Autos had been distributed to dealerships. Homes had been sold or closed up. Fuel was being produced again. Stores had the food they needed. Farmers had their equipment running.

Yes, people were still dealing with the grief of losing their family members. You can't put a clock on feelings. Memories will be there for a long time.

On the Village, the future is now. Bright is shining. Next comes exploring Amber.